NEVER SATISFIED

The Story of the Stonecutter

as told by **Dave Horowitz**

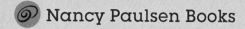

Nancy Paulsen Books

for Rachel, my rock!

NANCY PAULSEN BOOKS
an imprint of Penguin Random House LLC
375 Hudson Street
New York, NY 10014

Library of Congress Cataloging-in-Publication Data
Names: Horowitz, Dave, 1970– author, illustrator.
Title: Never satisfied : the story of the Stonecutter / as told by Dave Horowitz.
Description: New York, NY : Nancy Paulsen Books, [2018]
Summary: Relates the consequences of a stonecutter's foolish longing for power.
Identifiers: LCCN 2017019911 | ISBN 9780399548468 (alk. paper)
ISBN 9780399548475 (ebook) | ISBN 9780399548499 (ebook)
Subjects: | CYAC: Stonecutters—Folklore. | Folklore—China.
Classification: LCC PZ8.1.H86153 Nev 2018 | DDC 398.2 [E]—dc23
LC record available at https://lccn.loc.gov/2017019911

Manufactured in China by RR Donnelley Asia Printing Solutions Ltd.
ISBN 9780399548468
1 3 5 7 9 10 8 6 4 2

Design by Dave Kopka. Text set in ITC Lubalin Graph Std.
The art was done with construction paper, charcoal, and colored pencils.

Author's Note

Long, long ago, I wanted to make books. I wanted to write the words and I wanted to draw the pictures. I always felt it was what I was meant to do. But then after about fifteen years and over a dozen books, a funny thing happened: I didn't want to do it anymore. It was a hard way to earn a living, and I wanted to do something more important. So I went back to school and became a paramedic. One day, though, sitting at the station, I was talking to an older, wiser medic, and I told him how I came to be there. I told him what I just told you. He looked at me funny and asked if I'd ever heard of an old Chinese folktale called "The Stonecutter." He gave me the gist of the story you are about to read, and then he laughed.

I laughed too, and said, *That's pretty good . . . but what's it have to do with me?*

Oh, nothing. He smiled. *Nothing at all.*

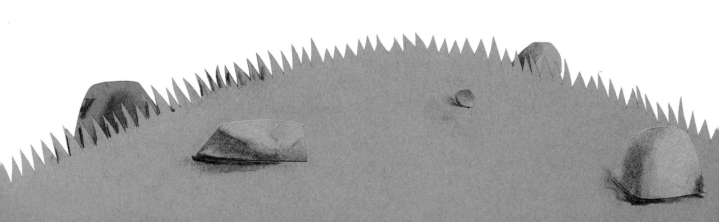

Once there was an old stonecutter named Stanley.

Stanley was good at his job, but cutting stone was a hard way to earn a living.

One day, on his way back from the rock quarry, Stanley noticed a businessman just sipping tea.

"Hmmf," said Stanley. "That
must be nice. I wish I were a
businessman."

And suddenly, to his great surprise, Stanley was transformed into a businessman.

He took a sip of tea and said, "Oh yeah! Now, *this* is more like it!"

But soon, outside his window, there was a wild commotion. It was the king!

"Wow!" Stanley said. "Now, that would be *really* nice! Man, I wish I were the king."

And again, suddenly—just like that—Stanley became the king. "This rules!" said Stanley. "I could get used to *this* kind of life!"

But before long, the sun beat down
on Stanley, and he grew weary.
He lowered his crown and said,
"Dude, I should be the sun! *Everyone*
would look up to me if I were the sun."

And to his great delight,

Stanley became the sun.

"Now, *this* is more like it!"

he said, beaming with joy.

But before long, a black cloud

appeared and darkened the sky.

"Oh, come on!" said Stanley.

"I didn't know *that* was a thing!

I should be the black cloud."

And of course, just like that, he was.

Being a black cloud suited Stanley. He let loose a mess of rain and lightning.

But soon there was a wind, a mighty wind. The wind pushed Stanley across the sky like he was nothing.

"Oh, come on . . ." said Stanley.

Well, you know what happened next. As soon as he decided that *he* should be the wind . . . Stanley became the wind.

"Now, *this* is what I'm talking about," said Stanley. "*Nothing* can stop me now!"

Until he came to a great stone.
Stanley huffed and puffed and blew
for all he was worth, but the stone
was unmoved.

"I SHOULD BE THE GREAT STONE,"
howled Stanley.

And of course, he became the great stone.

Finally, Stanley was satisfied. And nothing could *ever* change that . . .

. . . until the next day,
when there appeared
a young stonecutter.